Pirate Pete's GIANT Adventure

by **Kim Kennedy**
illustrated by
Doug Kennedy

Abrams Books for Young Readers
New York

"Hoist the sails!" shouted Pirate Pete. "Avast ye!"

"Wake up," squawked his parrot. "You're dreaming again."

Pete opened his eye. The parrot was right. They were still adrift at sea in their little rowboat. They were getting nowhere fast and Pete knew it.

"Oh, I wish I hads a ship!" moaned Pete. "Why, I'd do anything for a ship!"

Just then, the waves began to shimmer. In a splash of foam, a sea-fairy appeared. "I'll grant your wish for a ship," she offered, "if you go on a special quest."

"What might that be, little matey?" asked Pete.

"Go to Thunder Island," she said, "and find the Sea-Fairy Sapphire."

Pete had heard of the Sea-Fairy Sapphire. It was a magical stone that had been stolen from the Sea-Fairy Kingdom.

"Return the sapphire to the ocean," she instructed, "and you will be rewarded with a wondrous ship."

"I'll do it," agreed Pete. "But how will I find the Sea-Fairy Sapphire without a map?"

"Just follow the sound of thunder," said the fairy. "But beware, for thunder does not always come from clouds." Then she disappeared.

A brisk wind began to blow, and the little rowboat traveled swiftly. Soon, over the sound of the breeze, came the rumbling of thunder.

Pete laid a hand to his ear, then checked his spyglass.
"Land ho!" cried Pete. "Thunder Island, straight ahead!"

They had just come ashore when *BOOM! BOOM! BOOM!*
Claps of thunder rolled.

"'Tis coming from the other side of the island," said the
parrot. So off they marched through the palm trees, with Pete
banging coconuts and singing,

"When I finds the Sea-Fairy Sapphire,
I'll get me a ship of wonder.
All I gots to do
Is follow the sound of thunder."

By and by, they came to the heart of the island.

"What a strange-looking lagoon," said the parrot. "And with all this thundering, why does it never rain?"

BOOM! Another rumbling sounded. Pete picked up his pace and cried,

"When I finds the Sea-Fairy Sapphire,
I'll get me a ship of wonder.
All I gots to do
Is follow the sound of thunder."

BOOM! BOOM!
"'Tis getting louder," said the parrot. "We must be near."

Pete looked through his spyglass. He could see something sparkling on a hill up ahead.

"I sees it!" said Pete. "I sees the Sea-Fairy Sapphire!"

Soon they came upon a cave, and Pete stumbled in. He grabbed the glimmering blue jewel.

"Why 'twas easy!" Pete cried.

"Quick, throw it into the sea," said the parrot. "Then we'll get our ship!"

"Not so fast," said Pete. "This here is a magical wishing stone. Let's see what it can do."

Pete stared into the glittering stone and commanded, "Give me a treasure map to the world's greatest treasures." The stone glowed a bright blue, and in a swirl of sea mist, a map appeared. Pete tucked it into his coat.

"That's enough," said the parrot. "Throw the sapphire into the sea!"

"Another thing," Pete told the stone. "I want the world's mightiest sword!"

The sapphire glowed even brighter, and a splendid sword appeared.

"That's enough!" squawked the parrot. "Now throw the sapphire into the sea so we can get our ship!"

"All right," grumbled Pete. But as they left the cave, a terrific crash shook the ground. *BOOM! BOOM! BOOM!*

Pete and his parrot looked up, up, up.

"A giant!" The parrot flapped. "The thunder has been coming from a giant's big feet stomping about!"

"Aye," gulped Pete, looking up at the big brute. "So he's the scurvy dog that hornswaggled the sapphire from the sea-fairies!"

The giant caught a whiff of Pete and snatched him up.

"I knew I smelled a pirate!" he bellowed. "A stinky pirate!"

"Ar! Not as stinky as you be," growled Pete.

"Oh, but you're salty, too!" snarled the giant.

Suddenly, he saw the sapphire tucked in Pete's hand.

"Tryin' to sneak the sapphire from me, ay?" he grumbled.

The giant drew Pete even closer, so that Pete could smell the stink of old seaweed on his breath. "Do ye know what I do to sneaky pirates?"

"Nay," Pete said.

"I yank off their hooks!" roared the giant, shaking the ground with his mighty voice.

With the giant's fingers wrapped tightly around him, Pete knew there was no chance for escape. But perhaps he could *outsmart* him.

"Ye can yank off me hook if ye wish!" Pete said. "Ye can use it to catch a big mackerel fish, but just don't throw me in the sea!"

The giant blinked, a bit puzzled. "What? A pirate afraid of the sea?" He scratched his head. "Forget yer hook," the giant decided. "I'm going to pull off yer peg leg!"

"Ye can pull off me peg leg if ye like," said Pete. "Ye can use it as a toothpick, but just don't throw me in the sea!"

"I'll use it as a toothpick, all right!" snorted the giant. "After I eats ye, that is!"

"Ye can eats me if you please," said Pete. "Ye can boil me up in a big pot of pirate stew, but just don't throw me in the sea!"

"Ye really are afraid of that sea, aren't ye?" said the giant, a glint of mischief in his eyes. "Well then, how about a little swim?"

With that, the giant hurled Pete into the sky. Clinging tightly to the sapphire, Pete flew into the clouds and then back down to the sea, where he landed with a great splash.

Suddenly, the waves began to churn and bubble. Then, up from the deep, an amazing ship arose, with Pirate Pete aboard!

"You tricked me!" shouted the giant, as he plowed into the water and grabbed the ship's anchor.

"We're doomed!" squawked the parrot. "He's pulling us in!"

"The sapphire can't save you now!" The giant laughed.

"Nay," said Pete. *"But me mighty sword can!"*

Pete drew the shining sword, and with the slightest touch, its gleaming blade cut the chain. The ship was set free!

"Now for a bit of me own thunder!" Pete shouted. "Fire cannon!"

With a tremendous *BOOM!* a cannonball shot from the ship, sending the giant fleeing back to the shore.

Then, a mighty wind filled the ship's sails, and off she went, far and away from Thunder Island. The sea-fairies had fulfilled their promise indeed! Pete's new vessel was the most wondrous ship to ever sail the high seas!

"Fine sailin' weather," cheered the parrot.

"Aye," called Pete, unfurling his new treasure map. And with a gleam in his eye, he sang,

> "I found the Sea-Fairy Sapphire,
> And I got me a ship of wonder.
> I'm off again to distant lands,
> Where there's jolly good treasure to plunder!"

To Kim

To my lovely wife, Meredith, and my little skipper, Julian
—Doug

Designer: Vivian Cheng
Production Manager: Alexis Mentor

Cataloging-in-Publication Data has been applied for
and may be obtained from the Library of Congress.
ISBN 978-0-8109-5965-1

Printed and bound in Singapore
15 14 13 12 11 10 9 8 7 6 5 4

Abrams Books for Young Readers are available at special discounts when purchased in quantity for premiums
and promotions as well as fundraising or educational use. Special editions can also be created to specification.
For details, contact specialsales@abramsbooks.com or the address below.

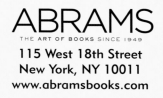

ABRAMS
THE ART OF BOOKS SINCE 1949
115 West 18th Street
New York, NY 10011
www.abramsbooks.com

Dec 2014
(2006)